T0120572

A Mother Torn...
Her Restoration

JOE D. JEFFERIES

WestBow Press books may be ordered through booksellers or by contacting:

WestBow Press
A Division of Thomas Nelson & Zondervan
1663 Liberty Drive
Bloomington, IN 47403
www.westbowpress.com
844-714-3454

All Scripture quotations are taken from the King James Version.

ISBN: 978-1-6642-3945-6 (sc)
ISBN: 978-1-6642-3944-9 (e)

Print information available on the last page.

WestBow Press rev. date: 06/30/2021

ONE

Helen Victoria Washington sat at the kitchen table nervously fidgeting her now warm cup of coffee. She looks up at the owl clock and groans, "John will be here in a few minutes. How do I tell him? What will he do"?

WHOSH!

"Uh!" Helen jumps. "The front door," she mumbles. Helen stands up. "I got to get him in the right mood."

She frowns. "There's no right mood for this." She balls tight fists under her chin and whispers, "I got to try." She conjures up a large smile and swung open the double doors. "John!" Helen and her smile plows through the double swinging doors. When she saw him, her smile pulls her lips between her teeth. Her throat locks.

"What's wrong with you?" John Lewis, her husband, asked.

Her hands began to wring together, her teeth still biting down on her lips.

He steps closer to her. "What is it? What's wrong?" Her eyes drips tears. He holds her hand, his other hand around her waist guiding her to the sofa. He smiles and asks rhetorically, "Is the sky falling, my wife?"

She swallows, preparing her throat to tell him. Not looking in his eyes, she says, "John, . . ."

Suddenly his smile is replaced by a frown. "Helen..."

"No John, don't say anything."

His head floods with negative thoughts; one thought painfully hovers in his brain: Is My wife having an affair? Should I come home from work and be told my marriage is over?

She continues, "I've been wanting to tell you for days . . ." she pauses. He grasps her shoulders with his large callous hands. "Tell, me! What is it?"

She cringes. "I can't!"

He keeps her shoulder in his hands. "Tell me, my wife!"

"John, promise me you will not be angry."

He drops his hands to his side. "I promise, Helen."

Through tear filled eyes she stares at him. "John, I have been sick for several days. I feel much better today.

So many, times I wanted to tell you."

John frowns, confuse.

"You promised you wouldn't angry."

He frowns harder. "What? . . . is it!" He asks through anticipation.

She covers her face with the palms of her hands. "I'm pregnant!"

His shoulders drop. "No! Not now. You know I wanted us to be married for at least four years before bringing a baby into the picture—we have only been married, uh, a year and a half."

"I know," she replies. "I wanted us to be financially set, too."

His eyes were glaring hard. "Baby! How could this happen? You were taking preventive measures."

"John, we are pregnant. I didn't do it alone."

John looks at her. "What happened."

"I ran out of birth control! I thought, maybe a few days wouldn't hurt."

"Helen, I guess it doesn't work like that? You would think it would."

She moves close to him. "John. Honey. My husband. I'm sorry."

"What's done is done." John says, "This will set us back, a little."

"The chances of getting pregnant were always there. It was not a one hundred percent deal. You knew that."

A tear is trapped on a few of her eye lashes—she blinks it off.

"Ok. Ok--" John sighs. He reluctantly reaches out his hands. "Okay."

She sees the lack of sincerity in his hands. Helen, with a cock brow steps back. More sincerely his hands jerks out, growing an inch or two.

"I'm happy for you."

"That's better." She smiles. "I said, we both are pregnant."

His smile fills his dirty face. "I'm happy for the both of us."

Her arms tighten around his dirty clothes. "That's better." He returns the hug. "You're dirty. Hug me like you mean it."

"The baby," he said, warningly.

"I'm only about two months pregnant." Still stuck in his arms, her head against his chest she says, "You know,

I've always prayed for two boys and a girl, and a husband like you to help me raise them."

"I remember. But let us wait a couple of years," said John. "You know, I was scared,"

"Scared? Scared of what?"

"Well. . ."

Helen's arms pulse a squeeze. "What?"

He looks away from her. ". . . that you were unfaithful."

She cranes her face to his and says, "John, how could you." She feels a blade in her heart. "What have I ever done to make you think that, or I would do such a thing?"

He sees the pain in her eyes and her face. "No Sweetheart, not you, you are a great wife. It's my insecurity."

"Why--?"

"Forget it--this is my first son."

"I guess it is best, since you agree it is to do with your thoughts. Only you can settle that. And do you think, you are moving too fast? It could be girl."

"Have you told your sister, yet? You know the husband is always the last to know."

"In most cases, yes. But you are about the fourth."

"The fourth!" He pushes back. "Who else knows?"

She smiles, pulls several napkins from its holder, and says, while wiping the grim from his shirt off her arms,

"Well, first, there's the doctor, the nurse, the receptionist, and finally, you. No. Barbara doesn't know."

"Good. The hospital does not count. And it's a boy."

"We'll see." She steps from him and sigh. "You know Barbara can't get pregnant. I hate to tell her."

"The both of you have just made up, after all those years. --lot of time lost. She is going to be an aunt. She might feel great. I think she is too tough to be hurt like that."

"I suppose you're right." She looks up at him. "John, I know we're having a hard time--your job cutting back.

I think now is the time to get a phone."

"Mm, ah, look, give it a few weeks, okay."

"Okay."

"Of course, I do have a large insurance policy," John said.

"I don't like it when you say that, now stop it."

"Okay, never again."

"That's what you said a couple of weeks ago."

Two

Seven months later, Helen is awakened by contractions. "John! John! Wake-up!" John lays there. She pushes him and screams, "John! Wake-up!"

He throws back the covers, jumps out of bed and runs. "Ooh! My toe!" He ran-hop back to the bedroom.

"Helen--?"

"John, it's time!" She forces a smile at his hopping. "For a minute I thought you were going without me. What happened in there? Why are you limping and hopping?"

"The desk." He wobbles to the closet and pulls out two tightly packed suitcases.

"John, where did that other suitcase come from? I'm not going there to stay."

"I thought you might need some extra things." He wobble-dash out of the bedroom, then the front door, and throws the two suitcases in the back of their brown and white station wagon. He runs back to help his wife to the car.

"What are you doing? No John! I'll feel better if I walk! Put me down."

"Ok." His lips between his teeth he eases his aching foot into his bedroom slipper.

"Is it that bad?"

"I think my pinky-toe broke when it hit the front room desk."

She pinches his cheek. "You get your pinky-toe checked out, ok."

He wipes her hand from his cheek. "I'm a man."

"Yeah. Next time you might bite your lips off. Well, let's hurry while the pain has eased up."

John bustles out the driveway, on the route he had practiced driving several times for this emergency.

"John! The potholes!" The pain had returned seconds ago.

"Ok. Ok." Pain grimaces his face as he presses the gas paddle.

"John! John!" She grips the rim of the back seat. "I didn't mean hit them!"

"I didn't know there were so many potholes in this road," he said. We're almost there." He looks up in the mirror. "Are you dialating?"

"Mm, dilating. Now drive!" Helen growls.

They pull into the emergency entrance of the Gaffney Memorial Hospital. He swings open the driver's door and ran-hop to the receptionist's desk.

"May I--"

"My wife's outside! In the baby! Car! She's having a baby!"

The receptionist, before he finishes explaining, was paging an intern.

Helen moans and groans as the interns lifts her, as gently as they could out the station wagon. John hops behind them.

"Will you--uh, get someone to check out my--uh, husband's foot," Helen says, trying to ignore her pains.

An intern looks back at John, then back at her. "He's a big boy. He will live. First, let us uncage someone—boy or girl?"

"Girl." Helen says as she puffs.

"Joining her, Big Guy?" the intern asked.

"Are you kidding? I couldn't take the films in the classes," John says while already holding his stomach.

Hours later John stands at Helen's bedside holding her hand.

One of Helen's eye lid drags halfway open and the other nearly close. "How's the baby?" she asked.

"She's fine. Up and running. The nurse just left. She said the Baby will be in here soon."

"Did they get the name right?" Helen's eyes had already begun to close.

"Yeah. Gravita Teresa, just like your great-grandmother's." Her eyes close.

THREE

Seven years later, 10:00am, Helen sat at the kitchen table with a hot cup of coffee, a ritual she began months before Gravita's birth. Helen gave a long sigh. She looks at her arms. "You two lone to hold my two sons. She looks up and says, "God, where are my two sons?" She nods. "Since Gravita, a loneliness I never expected is tearing at me. She's holding all the time I once held." She frowns. "I feel shame, jealous of Gravita, my daughter." She smiles. "Uh, of course, this is his first child, and I am glad to have been the woman."

She rubs her hand across the table, raking spilled sugar into a napkin. While balling the napkin in her hand she took a sip of coffee and slumps back in her chair and stars at the ceiling. "To lose another ounce of John's attention frightens me." She lightly braces the hot cup of coffee and swivels her head side to side, despairing and fighting a thought that is echoing in her head. *Maybe I should not have given birth to Gravita.*

A few days later, her ritual time, May 2006, Helen sat at the kitchen table with a cup of hot coffee. The central air unit humming near the kitchen window, and sirens blasting in the distant. For several seconds she listens to the sirens. "I pray no one is hurt," she mumbles. She stares into her almost empty cup. ". . . God, when?"

"Mama . . ."

"Uh!" Helen jumps, startled by her daughter. "What is it, Baby?"

"I need help with this one math problem."

Helen angles the book and looks at the math problem. "Sweetheart, you know I'm no good with math. Your father will be home, shortly."

"Yes, ma'am." Gravita left the kitchen.

"That girl even does schoolwork on teachers' workday. Helen pushes up from the table to refill her cup. Out the kitchen window an envious scene caught her eyes; a mother playing with her two sons--not school age yet. She turn from the window, fills her cup, and sat back down and stare at her coffee. She bit down on her bottom lip. Her eyes narrow as if listening to a small distant voice. She slaps her hands against the table as if she had gotten an answer from the voice. "Yes. Tonight's the night! I can feel it!" She watches the ripples of coffee vanish in the wall of the cup. She jumps. The doorbell had startled her. Who can that be? No salesman or woman." A joyful spring in her walk she enters the front room. The thought of conceiving tonight continues to dance in her head. With a large smile, not looking through the peephole she opens the front door. Her smile metamorphoses into some grotesque form. Her body is sucked into a horrifying dimension... she felt a convulsion in her stomach.

Two officers, their hats in their hands, their faces masked in sadness, stares at her.

The senior officer asks, "Mrs. Helen Washington?"

She could only stare. Her brown sugar complexion was blush. The sirens she had heard earlier reanimates in her head--then her husband. She wanted to scream "NO" for thinking what she is thinking. Then the infamous reality hit. Why are they here--hats in their hands?

The senior officer steps closer. "Mrs. Helen Victoria Washington?"

Her lips tremble open. "Ye-yes."

The officer inhales deeply, squares his shoulders, resenting this moment, asks, "May we come in?"

Without a word her weaken legs steps back. She carries her heavy body to the sofa. The junior officer helps her sat on the sofa.

"We believe your husband was in a fatal accident, about forty minutes ago. We're sor--"

"Catch her!" The junior officer yelled.

The senior officer grabs her before her head hit the table. They lay her on the sofa.

"Mrs. Washington. Mrs. Washington. Are you ok?" asked the senior officer.

Her eyes open slowly. "No." She struggles up.

The senior officer holds her arm. She jerks her arm from him. After sitting up, she presses her fingers against both sides of her head as if ministering to a migraine.

"...anything we can do?" the senior officer asked.

She looks up through her fingers at the officer, then at his nametag. "Officer Shane, you are not sure that is my husband, are you? He should still be at work." She knew he have been getting off early since the cut back of work. Then she notices a white cloth wrapped around a lump in Officer Shane's hand.

He notices her stare at the handkerchief. He peels it open and hands it to her. Her hand jitters out. She jerks her hand back but could not pull her eyes from the charred wallet.

"You recognize it?" Officer Shane asked.

Helen nods.

"This and the tag are all the identification we could retrieve for now." Officer Shane says, "We're sorry, Ma'am. We will get this back to you after the investigation. We'll see our way out."

"Officer--"

Officer Shane turns.

She thought about the debts they are in and his joking about his life insurance. Suicide. He could not have meant it any other way. "How did it happen?"

"An eyewitness said he dodged a squirrel and lost control of the vehicle and hit the tree."

"A squirrel!" Helen drops back into the sofa.

The junior officer turns to her. "You still must come and claim the body. Someone will contact you. Procedures Ma'am." The door closes with a long whoosh.

"Mama. . ."

Helen quickly, the best she could, pull herself together.

"Who was that?"

Helen couldn't let Gravita see she's crying. "How can I tell my daughter her father is dead?" She heard steps going toward the window. "OH," Helen shouts. Gravita stops. "Sweetheart, get mama a glass of water." She could not let Gravita see the police car. Helen runs to her bedroom, lock the door, falls face down on her bed. "Why! Why! Why! Why did--"

Tat-tat-tat. Steps stops at the bedroom door.

"Mama, your water."

"Leave it near the door," she said in a calm voice. Helen listens for Gravita's steps--there was none. She know her daughter is near the door and knows something is not right. Helen buries her face in her bed. In low whispers

she moans, "What will come of our lives now? My daughter is waiting for her father to come and help her with her math." Helen sits up in anger. She hears Gravita's steps going to her room. Helen's words were louder. What about my prayers to you. Ever since I was a little girl, I prayed to you, two boys and a girl." Helen angrily rolls off her bed. She grabs a wad of the comforter and jerks it off the bed. She frowns at the black sheet. The black sheet flies to the other side of the room like a black cloud. "I'll never believe in another prayer." She raises her hands over her head--balled fists—they tremble as they tighten. She holds her hands back from knocking everything off her dresser. "And you." Her hands drop to her sides. Her eyes still on her dresser. She wants to strike out at something, but she knew Gravita would hear it.

She stares--

A week later after the funeral Gravita runs across the black carpet, and lay her head in her mother's lap and ask the same question she have already asked many times, "Mama, when is Daddy coming home?"

No reply. Only a smile and a hug from her mother. Gravita looks up at her mother. Helen's mouth opens to explain, but Gravita's light brown eyes are like looking into the two most beautiful ponds anyone could behold, never to be polluted by ripples of pain or the redness that now, so often, encage them, but in them, Helen could see John. They stare at each other for several seconds. Helen starts to tell her. Helen's lips trembles. Helen smiles and gives Gravita a hug, which always seem, for a short while, fill some of the void in her daughter.

Gravita gently pulls from her mother's arms, and runs to the picture window and stands behind half the curtain, where she would stand for hours, watching every car that drive by, hoping that an old brown and white station wagon would pull into the driveway with her father's face behind its windshield. The brown and white station wagon never comes.

Tears trace Helen's cheeks as she watches Gravita stare expectantly out the window. Helen bites down on her bottom lip and steps toward her daughter to tell her, to end her daughter's agony, something she should have done two weeks ago. Helen stops. She whispers almost under her breath, "How can I tell her? Her father will never come home. He will never help her with her math, never tuck her in bed--a kiss, goodnight." A chime ripples through the house, startling Helen. She realizes it is the doorbell. Helen wipes her cheeks and open the door.

"Aunt Barbara!" Gravita screams.

"Hi, Baby." Barbara stoops down and gives Gravita a hug. "Baby, you've been crying?"

Gravita stares at the floor.

"Gravita, go to your room," Helen said. She knows her sister is going to preach to her again.

Barbara grabs Helen's hand. "Helen, I got to talk to you." She pulls Helen into the kitchen. "Helen, when are you going to tell her?" Barbara lavern Sneakly asked. "It's been two weeks. She has the right to know."

"Barbara, I've tried many times to tell her, even just now, but every time I look into those light brown eyes, I see her father and I know the pain it will cause her."

"She's seven years old. It will not kill her. It is not like you need to tell her how horrible the accident was. Helen . . ." Barbara points toward the front room. "Each time I drive pass this house that child is standing in the same spot, like a stature, staring out that window!"

"I know. I'm not . . ."

"Wait, I'm not finished yet!" Barbara folds her arms. "You are looking out for Helen. You do not want Helen to feel any pain."

"But I do feel pain. . ."

"Not like hers. You can end hers. She does not deserve this. Cut her pains short, or I will. Tell her, or I will."

The kitchen's woodened chair crackles when Helen flops

down in it, her arms fold and her eyes filled with tears. "I know I'm not as strong as you. As far back as I can--"

"Cut it short, Helen! You know that has nothing to do with this."

"Yes, it does."

"You're not going to get out of this. You need to tell her one day--why not now. If you are thinking about waiting till you think she is old enough she might hate you for not telling her sooner. Tell me, what would you have accomplished?"

Silence.

Helen stares at the floor, not able to bear Barbara's authoritative glare.

"You . . ."

"Ok, ok." Helen cut Barbara short. "You're right. You are always right! I will talk to her. Now, can I finish what I was about to say?" Helen's stare was still on the black and white tiled floor. Childlike, Helen places each foot in a square and raise her heels up and down several times.

Barbara's lips lines at Helen's childish demeanor. She put her hands on her large hips. She is big bonded from their father's side of his family and Helen medium from their mother's side of her family, and more attractive than Barbara. "Yes, yes. Go right ahead Helen. I'm all ears."

"Like I was trying to say, as far back as I can remember I've always respected you. I wanted to be like you, strong, and always right. Mom and Dad would ask you for advice. Sometimes I would rush to my big sister's room, even though I knew I might get a whipping for it. I would put on her shoes and primp my hair like hers and prance in front of her full-length mirror." She looks up at Barbara with moist eyes. "I remember as if it was yesterday."

"I-I didn't know you felt that way about me." Barbara steps closer to Helen. "From the time I was a teen and you were twelve when we fell out over some raggedy doll that belonged to me. You were so angry. We just buried our differences about three years ago. I thought you disliked me and everything I stood for.

"I remember that. You had let me keep it for so long. I guess I wanted to win something over you. To defeat you in something."

"Ahh. You have defeated me in something."

Helen cocks a wondering-brow.

"Gravita." Barbara said. "Now take care of her, ok."

Helen smiles. "I guess what I'm trying to say is that I respect you and wish I have your strength. I am glad to have a sister like you to push me -- in somethings. And I thank you and Daniel for watching her when I work on Saturdays."

Her and Barbara walks back into the front room. Barbara sat in the blue crushed velvet recliner, and Helen sat in the blue crushed velvet love seat facing Barbara.

"Helen, you should step out more. Get your license, and a car--"

She interrupted Barbara. ". . . somethings, remember. I'll talk to her this evening."

Barbara's lips stretch into a frustrating line. She got the hint that Helen didn't want her meddling in that part of her life. Barbara lifts herself out the recliner. "I gotta go. Gotta get supper ready for Daniel. My turn to cook. I'll check on you tomorrow to see if you kept your word."

Helen props an elbow on the arm of the love seat, her fingers holding her forehead. "I said I would," Helen said

"Ok. Ok. I'll see myself out. Bye, bye, Gravita, Sweetheart," Barbara yelled out.

Later that evening Helen sat down and calls her daughter from the window and signals her to climb in her lap. She turns Gravita's back to her. She knows she will not tell her if she got one glance into Gravita's eyes. "Sweetheart, Mommy has something to tell you."

"Mama, why are you sad? Anything wrong? You miss Daddy, too? Daddy will be home soon, tonight. I know he will." Gravita's eyes lit-up. "You told me if I pray for good things God will give them to me. I prayed real hard last night, and when Aunt Barbara was here.

Gravita's faith in her father's return stabs Helen's heart. Helen's words tremble out, "Baby--" she squeeze Gravita tight. "your Daddy" --tighter-- "won't be coming home."

The house became a vacuum; time froze; darkness fills the house.

Helen hears her daughter's voice rattle as it forces out the question, "Why Daddy never coming home?"

Helen feels another sword pierce her heart--she jolt as if it was cold steel.

Gravita turns--Helen quickly twists her back around.

"Why is *my* Daddy never coming back home?" Her tears drip on her mother's coiled arms. Everything is a ghostly image to Gravita. "Did Daddy leave us?"

Helen's words clung in her throat.

"Randy, in my class, his daddy left him, and he cries almost every day."

"No, Sweetheart, your Daddy would never leave us. He loved us too much. He still does."

"Then, why Daddy won't come home?"

Again, she squeezes her daughter. Her tears soak the back of Gravita's long black hair.

"Mama, I want my Daddy. Bring him back home."

"No Sweetheart."

"Why? Don't you love Daddy anymore?" Silence fills the house except for Gravita's deep breathing, increasing with each breath. Then, as if her lungs explode, she screams, "You ran Daddy away!"

"No Baby."

"They said Randy's mom ran his daddy away."

"No Baby--" "--let me go! Let-me-go!" She tries to rip her mother's arms from around her. "You ran my Daddy away!"

"No, Baby!"

"Let me go! Let me go!"

"Your Daddy was in an accident!" Helen finally disgorged.

Gravita's insides derails--she froze. She wipes her face and eyes. "Daddy in the hospital?" She looks at her mother. "Can we go see Daddy? I haven't seen my Daddy in a long time."

Helen, seeing her daughter's world *torn* and no force could repair it. Holding back her outburst of crying, her body jolts like small explosions ripping through her. She manages to say, "Baby, I'm sorry. Your Daddy is . . .d-dead."

Gravita's lungs froze full. She stares into nothing for several seconds. She exhales. "Mama, they buried Daddy. We won't ever see Daddy again?"

"Yes Baby. We will see him again."

"When?"

"In heaven Baby, when you go there."

Gravita twists around, her knees in her mother's lap. She wraps her arms around her mother's neck and buries her face deep under her mother's jaw. "Mama," she cries, "I want my Daddy. I want to go to heaven now, to see Daddy."

"You will, Baby."

"When can I go? I want to see my Daddy, now!"

"Oh, Sweetheart. . ." She lifts Gravita's head until their eyes were level. "You will."

"When?"

"Very soon, Baby." She knows she is a bad teacher about God and life after death. She stopped believing in God after John's death. How can Gravita live without her father, Helen thought? "Come with Mama." She stood up with Gravita in her arms. "I know your Daddy is waiting for you."

The next day Barbara knocks several times on Helen's door. No one Came. Barbara leans and looks in the window. She sees no one. She pushes the doorbell several times. "Come on Helen, I got some cooking to do. The door jerks open.

"Hi. I was sleeping. I was wondering who is knocking and pushing the doorbell like that."

"Sorry about that. I wanted to get here before Gravita left for school If she went today. To see if you kept your promise."

"I told her. It was hard, but I did it. I also had to explain to her about death and heaven."

"Something you should've done a long time ago," Barbara says.

"We prayed together. I told her that her father is in heaven, and her prayers goes to heaven, and he would hear them."

Barbara stare at Helen. "Now, what about her?"

Helen folds her arms and frisk them as if to knock off a chill. "It tore something inside her--I felt it, as if I heard it. I know she'll never be the same." She throws her arms down. "Time will tell. And I did give her the choice to stay home, but she chose to go to school." Helen smile and continue, "She sure has your strength. I guess she was meant to be your child."

Barbara fidget as if she is being mocked, and then says, "Neither of you will ever be the same. I think she should see a child psychologist. I think you should see someone as well."

"I don't know. That sounds so--."

"Liberal," Barbara snaps. "I still think you should."

Helen nod. "We'll be ok."

"Ok. I'll stop right here. Do it your way. I'm glad you told her." Barbara looks at her watch. "I'm home if, you need anything."

Helen walks Barbara to the door. They hug.

Four

Nine years later, two months after Gravita's sixteenth birthday, she for the third weekend asks her mother, "May I go out with my friend?"

"Mm, huh?"

Gravita moves to the sink and fills a glass with water. "Mama, may I go to Shirley's birthday party?"

Helen stops chopping cabbage, slaps the knife on the counter, and turns to Gravita. "Gravita, I know your best friend Shirley, and I have told you over and over to pick another best friend."

Gravita scrunch her eyes. "Mama why are you always downing her. You don't know her." Gravita angry, pushes away from the sink. "Why?"

"Young lady, what has gotten into you? You don't talk to me in that tone."

Helen steps closer to her.

"Mama, I'm sixteen, and I do have some rights. We're taught that in school, you know."

Helen steps closer, almost toe to toe. "The answer is still, no."

Gravita steps back and impudently looks away from her mother.

Her insolent attitude pour fuel on the flame of Helen's anger. She points at Gravita--her finger nearly touching Gravita's face. "The only rights you have right now, is to go to your room, and no lips!"

Gravita toss the glass in the metal dual sink. The glass shatter on the border of the dual sink; she storms for the swinging doors.

"Don't you walk out those doors! Come back here and pick up this glass! And sweep up every piece of it. What have gotten into your head, child?"

"You told me to go to my room!"

Helen held Gravita's arms as they hung down her sides. Helen extinguished her anger. Her hands gently Caress Gravita's arms. "Sweetheart, this is not you."

"Mama, I have grown up." She squints at her mother's hands. "All my friends get to go out when they are sixteen--some even younger." She shook her mother's hands from her.

Helen's anger flames. "I'm not your friends' mother. And, as long, as you are my child and live under my roof, you'll do as I say." Helen points at the sink and floor. "Now clean it up and go to your room."

After cleaning up the glass Gravita rush out the kitchen.

In anger Helen groan to herself. "Five days a week, sometimes on Saturdays I take a taxi back and forth to work, trying to make a living for both of us.

The front door ease open and shut with the same accuracy.

Gravita knocks on her Aunt Barbara's door.

"Who is it?" Barbara's voice bore through the door.

"Gra--Gravita."

Barbara rush to the door and jerks it open. "Gravita, why are you crying? What is wrong? Come in and tell Aunt Barbara."

They sat on the sofa holding hands.

"Sweetheart, stop crying and tell me what's wrong."

Gravita pulls out a few napkins from the napkin holder and blot her eyes and nose. "I'm sixteen, and for weeks I have asked Mama to let me go out with my friends. I'm not going to do anything bad--only relax and have fun." Most of Gravita's words were broken sobs.

Barbara stands up. "Come baby. Go wash your face. You should not Let people see your weakness. We are going to talk to your mother."

Barbara had always been a person who love to be in control. Her high School friends called her, 'Miss. Control Freak'. All her dates only lasted a few weeks, except with Daniel, her husband. She, to this day do not understand why he married her--maybe because he is the only person that sees right through her.

Barbara's '99 Oldsmobile pulls into Helen's driveway. Barbara storms her way into Helen's house. "Helen!

Helen!"

Barbara screams shock, Helen. Helen runs out the kitchen and into the dining room. She froze. She stares at Gravita standing behind Barbara. The door squeaks' made Helen squint. She stops the door and moves close to Gravita and Barbara.

"Gravita--"

Helen cuts Barbara short. "Oh, don't knock, just barge on in!"

Barbara grabs Helen's hand and pulls her toward the den.

Helen jerks her hand free. "We can talk right here."

Barbara threw her purse on the sofa, put her hands on her hips, and beams dominate eyes at Helen. "Gravita came to me in tears and--"

". . . hold it!" A hard frown warps Helen's face. Before you go any farther. This is my daughter. I do things the way I wants. Not by the ways of an outsider."

"Outsider! Outsider!" Barbara leans back on one leg. "Now I'm an outsider."

"Yes! The moment you teamed up with my daughter to go against my demands, you became an outsider."

Silence fills the front room. Then some muffle tapping sounds.

Gravita watch her aunt, waiting for her to reply in her defense. Barbara only stands there with fold arms. Her right foot drumming the black carpet. Helen's ability to standup for herself shocks Barbara, especially against her.

Gravita is stun, seeing her aunt, a person she always known to be strong, rock solid, now is stall in time, speechless. Gravita stomps. "But Mama!"

"...who told you to leave? You were supposed to be in your room. Go!" Helen points toward Gravita's bedroom.

Gravita looks at her aunt, then her mother, and then the floor and storms to her room. The door slams behind her.

"Helen, there's no reaching you, are there? I've seen all I need to see."

"And what does that mean, Big Sister?" Helen squint as her mind booms back in time. Back to the rag doll, and the many times she was punished for entering her big sister's room.

"I don't know, Helen."

"If you are into reruns, just stay tune on this channel." Helen cocks a brow.

Barbara jerks her head, grabs her purse, and treks to the front door. Before stepping outside, she turns and yells, "Gravita, bye baby." Barbara slams the front door shut.

Helen kicks the door.

Again, Helen and Barbara have a wall of anger between them. Betrayed by her daughter emanates much anger in her. She battles the flow of anger. She knows a mother should never feel what she is feeling toward her. daughter. She storms to Gravita's bedroom. The door flies open starling Helen. Gravita grazes her mother's leg with her suitcase as she passes her mother.

"Child . . .! And where do you think you're going?"

"I have a name." Gravita jerkes the front door open.

"You are too smart for this and you're making a mockery of it."

"I didn't ask to be smart."

"Child, if you take one step out that door, don't you ever think about coming back here, you hear me."

Not looking back Gravita says, "Loud-and-clear, Helen." She

stops and turns. "Maybe, just maybe if you had told me sooner about Daddy, I wouldn't be this way—you didn't even take me to the funeral." She walks back to her mother and leans her tear-ripped face close to Helen's. "I still hold memories of the days I stood in" –she points-- "that window." Gravita jerkes from her mother and rushes out the door.

Helen watches Gravita speed walk across the lawn, kicking up dried grass that was cut yesterday. Speechless, Helen falls against the door jamb. Her mind flies back to Gravita standing, day after day, for hours behind the curtains waiting for her father. She whispers, "Baby, I'm sorry. Barbara, you were right, she does hate me for not telling her." She pushes from the door jamb. "But I still can't let you hang out like that. We will get past this baby. I know we will."

Three weeks later Helen pounds the arms of her chair until her fists ache. She could no longer detain the crave to see her daughter. She waits till it is near Gravita's bedtime and then hurries to Barbara's house. In the shadow of a large maple in front of Barbara's house she stares in her sister's picture window. Helen's heart jump when she saw Gravita in her robe. Helen's arms reach out to her daughter. "Come home, Baby." She hugs herself—she needed to fill them with something.

Supported against the maple tree Helen says, "I can't give in. If I give in now, it will never stop. John would never allow it." She inhales and looks up as if getting praises from John. "Neither will I." She pushes from the tree and lugs herself away. Several steps later she stops in the shadow of another maple and looks back to Barbara's house. "Do I really know what's best for my daughter?"

Vexed, she looks up into the maple. "Hold it, old gal, you just trying to find a reason to go running to her, asking for forgiveness--blaming yourself; the easy way out, yet a bigger price to pay, in-full." She looks back at Barbara's house. "I am sorry I didn't tell you, sooner. You are using that against me to justify your actions. All this is about you being part of the herd. Getting out with your friends." Helen turns and continues home, yet the pain of loss rips through her. It is my fault. I should had told you. Her steps slow down. How can I change the past? I must not give into her. "Oh, my. This is a long walk," she says, trying to make herself feel better and searching for rest from the weight of her *torn* moments. "I guess I should have taken John's many advices and gotten my driver's license." She remembered what he sometimes jokingly said; 'Look out rest of the drivers, here comes Mustang Helen'. "Oh John, I wish you were here. He is not here. Pull yourself together. Face it, sister, you are in this alone. God has deserted you.

If there is a God." Those mumbling drain her strength even more—a heaviness—the same heaviness she would feel each time she would question, is there a God. She looks up. She could not hold back from saying, "God, you never heard my prayers or seen my dreams." She looks down and nods. "If you did, and you are there, how could my life come to this. Is this *love*? Where are my two sons? Where is the husband to help me raise them? You took him away from me. Now my daughter."

Helen is confused. All her life she was told there is a God. And all her life till John's death she believed that. Her marriage, at least she thought so, was only a few degrees from being perfect. She is trap between real and fantasy.

FIVE

Six weeks later Helen receives a subpoena to appear in court; The word CUSTODY stung her eyes. She is feeling her legs floating from under her. She palms the wall and everything in her reach for support as she lugs toward her bedroom. Again, she falls face down on her bed. She cries herself to sleep.

A few hours later she jumps up, panting, sweating, and engulfed by darkness, except for the green film of light, from the digital clock on her nightstand. She balls portions of the sweaty sheet in her hand. "I will not cry, anymore. I will stand my ground. The court will be on my side." She squeezes her fingers into tight fists, tighter, tighter, 'til her Wrist throbs. "I am her mother. She's my child." She opens her hands. The small finger of her right hand is cramped--in a daze she straightens it with her other hand. "Baby, please, come home."

SIX

A month later Helen is sitting wounded in a Cherokee County courtroom. Helen, every now and then, looks across the courtroom at her daughter and Barbara. They never look her way.

After over half of the cases in court had been tried the tense moment was born.

"Gravita Teresa Washington and Barbara Lavern Sneakly," the District Attorney voices in the courtroom.

"Very sneaky," Helen says.

Gravita and Barbara stands up.

"Come forward, please," the DA says.

Helen watches them walk down the aisle with their heads high and straight.

"Helen Victoria Washington," the DA calls.

Helen stands up. "Here."

"Come forward, please."

After they were sworn in the DA address the matter to the court.

After forty-minutes of battling, Helen lost Gravita to Barbara as her legal guardian.

Helen is charged being too strict on her daughter and not allowing her to come back home. The judge also based his decision on the fact that Gravita is old enough to make the decision to whom she may live with, and that she is an A-B student and has never been in trouble with the law, or in school--a model student.

The court's decision crush Helen. She faints. Helen spent two days in the Gaffney Memorial Hospital. Neither Gravita nor Barbara came to see her.

The evening of the second day Helen is discharged from the hospital. She steps out a taxi and onto her driveway. Helen stands in the driveway, staring at her house. "How can I go in there. All that I love are taken from me." She folds her arms around her torso—her chest squeezing her heart and lungs—her stomach churning.

She looks toward Barbara's house. "I will never speak to you again. I curse the day we made-up." Walking across the concrete driveway, her stomach feels as if eating itself. Her shoulders toward the ground. She, walks as what she thought a condemned man would, when walking death row: his consolation is, his will be over in minutes. She growls aloud, "Mine will last a lifetime."

She lugs herself inside her house--not a home.

ALONE . . .No longer a Home.

Seven

Two weeks later, one Saturday night Gravita's crying face woke Helen. She sat up and rolls to the edge of her bed and open the curtains. She stared into the two large vertical rectangle panes. Her image is trapped in one of the panes, then incinerates by the headlights of a passing car, then reincarnates. She stares at her ghostly reflection. "I wonder if Gravita is out with her friends." She places a hand over her lips when she notices her lips moving with her thoughts. Helen falls back across her bed.

Helen jumps up. She feels another presence in the house. Suddenly, her breath locks. Unconsciously, she is standing up. Her breath unlocks—breathing deep--expectantly. "My Baby! She's home!" Helen rushes to Gravita's room. Gravita's door was shut as it had been since she left. Then reality set in; my baby is not home. Helen is still afraid to open the door--she have not been in there since Gravita left--she tried but could not. Finally she reaches out and grabs the doorknob. With her eyes shut she cracks the door and stands there smelling the sweet fragrances of Gravita's perfumes.

The door pulls from her hand--Gravita's presence returns--the door stop against the chair behind it. Helen's eyes pop open. Her heart sputters when she saw, in the dark, a black silhouette of Gravita sitting on her bed, reaching out to her, saying, "Mama! Help me, please! Please, Mama!" She rushes to her daughter, wraps her arms around Gravita, slicing through her. Like an evil mist Gravita slowly dissipates. "Noooooo!" Helen sat up in bed screaming, her hands beating the green film of light, searching for her daughter. "My Baby! My Baby!" Helen jumps out of bed and scrambles to Gravita's room. She slaps the light switch--the room aglow. Gravita was not there.

Helen raised her fists over her head and cries, "Oh, God! If you are here, what is going on? Why do you hate?

Why play tricks on me?" She drops on Gravita's bed. The doorbell chimes. She jumps up and looks at the clock concealed in a glass pyramid on Gravita's vanity and walks lifeless to the door. "I can't handle another disappointment. Who is at my door at this hour?" Her teeth grind together. "This better not be Barbara." Deep in her head she could hear, I pray it is my daughter. She did not want to hear it. She peeps through the peephole. She is thrown back in time—a time she never wants to experience again. She fumbles with the lock--finally the door opens, but only as far as the safety-chain would allow it.

"Mrs. Helen Washington? Mrs. Helen V Washington?" the officer asks, melancholy.

". . . y-yes. I am." Her voice trembles. She presses crossed arms to her chest as if to hold her body together. She could feel herself passing out. She doesn't want to know why the officer is in here house. She wants to go backwards in time, far beyond her pains--back to her childhood. She knows why the officer is in her house.

The officer stares into her black sunken eyes; they are really dark brown. For several seconds they only stare at each other. Then the officer shifts his eyes to the chain lock, signaling her to remove it. She closes the door. Her hand quake out of control. The chain falls, sways side to side like a pendulum of death. The door is heavy in her hands.

The officer is dismay. He senses she might faint if he tells her, her daughter is dead. The rookie tilts his head to one side and said into his lapel mic, "I need paramedics' assistance at 414 West Jefferies Street."

"What are you doing? I don't need any paramedics." She sat on the sofa and weaves her fingers together. ". . . I've been here before." Her countenance is hollow, her whole world is hollow.

"Cancel the paramedics," the rookie officer says in his mic. "Mrs. Washington, everything is going to be okay."

She cut her eyes at the officer.

He could feel the gravity from the weight that lays on her.

Everything is going to be okay. Everything is going to be okay. Those words hammer her brain. The anger she is holding against the world she momentarily directs it at the officer.

Her voice crackle, "Officer." She stars at the black carpet. "Save yourself the trouble."

The rookie sighs. He knew they made a mistake sending him. No experience for such a tense situation.

"My daughter is . . . de . . . dead." She gasps several times, stands up, labors to the window, and stands in the same spot Gravita had stood many times waiting for her father. Irony. Helen is torn farther from God. Her daughter's tortured pass haunts her. Her lips move without words. She is now her daughter. I am sorry Baby. I should have told you sooner.

The rookie leans forward. "Ma'am--?"

She jerks the curtains close and labors back to the sofa. "Now tell me, officer, what happened, and don't call me ma'am."

He clears his throat and sits in the black loveseat across from the sofa. He looks at his watch. --3am--. "Ah, two hours ago, at a club named Ponytail" --the officer grits his teeth-- "she was sh-shot."

Helen tense--an icy hand scrapes down her spine--her fingers curls tight. She squints, a squint that empties her world, nothing else to care for. She does not know why she asks the next question or why she would want to know. All she knows is that she wanted to know. "Where--" she looks at his nametag. "Was she shot, Officer Phelps?"

He fidgets. ". . . the head, Ma', Mrs. Washington."

Helen stared into nothing. Her fingers curls into tight fists, feeling Barbara's in them.

"Mrs. Washington. Mrs. Wash. . . ."

Before he could, she gave a large gasp as if she had just

overcome suffocation. "I'm okay, officer." She sat up taller. "You know, about that time I had a dream that was so real. I saw my daughter."

Officer Phelps squint. "... in her room." Helen mindlessly plays with her fingers. ". . . she, . . . she was reaching out to me. Begging me to help her." She put her hands over her face. "I couldn't help her! I could not help Gravita." She stands up and walks to the door.

Officer Phelps looks at her. He could see the callous veil that seals her. He knows nothing else can hurt her. His mouth opens.

"I'll be ok," she says before he could speak. "Like I said, I've been here before." The door is weightless in her hands. It drifts close behind the officer.

EIGHT

Helen enters Gravita's room, picks up a sock dropped from Gravita's rapid packing, and holds it to her mouth and nose. Her tears crawl into the sock. Then she lifts Gravita's picture from the chest of drawers.

"Oh Baby . . ." Helen bellows several times. The doorbell blasts. Her grief magnifies the chimes to an irritating level. She storms to the door. "I don't need another officer telling me my daughter is dead."

Barbara, in tears stands on the other side of Helen's door.

Helen looks through the peep hole. Her heart flutters, her head swells with anger. Her hands rocket to the Lock, the chain lock sways like a pendulum. Helen's lips mimic several times, *I'll kill her! I'll kill her!* Helen jerks the door open.

"Helen . . .! Helen . . .!"

Before Helen knew it, she slaps her sister. Helen grits her teeth, holding back the claws of anger that craves revenge. "Go! Get off my property!"

"But Helen . . .!" Barbara rubs her stinging jaw.

"Don't you say another word, you, sneaky . . . You killed my daughter. I curse the day you and I made peace. I never want to see you again." Helen steps close to her. Her fists trembling over Barbara's head.

Barbara coils like a frighten child. "Helen--"

"No! Quiet! If it wasn't for you." Her fist tightens. ". . . Gravita would still be alive."

Barbara slump, nearly dropping to her knees. Helen's words stab deep, ripping the sinew that holds Barbara's slump body together. Barbara knees is like over cooked noodles--she grabs the metal support rail.

Helen continues, "You can't have a child, so you took mine. You killed her. Now GO! You killed my baby! When I said she was meant to be your child, I didn't mean steal her from me. I said, Go!"

Barbara stumbles backward. 'You killed her.' 'You killed my baby!' batters Barbara's mind. She turns and runs, leaving her car in Helen's driveway. Barbara overshot her walkway and trips over her sprinkler. Daniel Bernard Sneakly hears her crying and tumbling on the ground. He rushes outside. "Barb, what's wrong? What has happened?" He looks around. "Where's the car?" He is afraid that she may have been in an accident. He examines her body.

"Daniel, Daniel, I'm sorry. Gravita. . . Helen, she. . ."

Daniel reasoned what have happened. He picks her up. "Come to bed. You can't change any of this."

In their bed, Daniel lays next to Barbara, listening to her mumble, "Gravita, Gravita, Helen. . ." Barbara babbles herself to sleep.

Daniel jumps up. He had fell asleep. Barbara's side of the bed is empty. "Barbara," he calls. No answer. Daniel rushes through the house calling her name. No answer. His rush became frantic. He rushes to the front door, unlocks it, and swung it open. He runs to the sidewalk. He turns in circles, looking for her. No Barbara. He rushes back in the house and sat on the edge of the bed.

"Maybe she has gone to get the car," he mumbles. He notices a light under the bedroom's bathroom door. He turns the doorknob. "Barbara! Barbara! Unlock the door." No reply. "Barbara, open the door!" Still no answer. He hammers the door with his fists. Still no answer. He backs up a few feet and rams his 6'2", 240lb body into the hollow veneer paneled door, cracking it down the middle, forcing the latch from the door jamb. The impact distort his vision. An image he didn't want to believe bar his fuzzy vision. The clearer his vision got, the more morbid the image. His vision rectifies. His wife hanging from her rob belt tied to the light fixture, partially ripped from the ceiling. He quickly climbs the counter and frees her belt.

He examines her body. He read the note pinned to her rob; *'I love you, Daniel.* He fumbles out the bathroom, through the house and out the front door.

Hammering on Helen's door startles her. Helen rushes from Gravita's bedroom. "This better not be Barbara, again--beating my door like that."

Helen's anger throbbed in her head. She fumbles to unlock the door. She swung it open. "Look, I . . ." Helen froze. "Daniel! Daniel, what are you doing here at this hour? What's wrong with you? I thought you were Barbara."

He thrust in knocking her to one side.

"Daniel!"

The springs in the sofa explodes when he drops on it. "She's dead! She hung herself!"

A glacial chill encages Helen. Then a desert heat consumes the chill. Her knees weaken. She drifts onto the floor in front of Daniel. He slides from the sofa to his knees. With blur visions they hug each other.

Helen pushes from him. "How could she? She's so strong. Yes, I know Gravita's death hurt her. And the way I came off on her. . ." Helen stands up. "I-I can't believe she hung herself."

"She had hurt a lot the whole time. Too many nights before we went to sleep, she asked, 'did I do the right thing'. I had no answers." He looks west toward his house. A dark stare.

Helen's eyes freeze on him.

He turns to Helen. "After y'all mother died she spent several months in the hospital. A nervous breakdown."

Daniel sigh. "Strong, no."

Helen frowns. She moves closer to him. He still on his knees. She places a hand on his shoulder.

"I'm sorry, I didn't know."

Holding her hand, he stands up. "She didn't want anyone to know. She wanted everyone else to believe she is invincible."

She pulls her hand from him. For several seconds no one spoke.

"You haven't called 911?" Helen asks.

"Can I call from here? I don't think I could ever go back in that house."

"I've never had a phone."

Daniel presses both arms against his stomach, releasing a deep sigh. "I can't go back in there."

Helen's eyebrows grew close together. She steps close to Daniel and holds his hands. "Whatever went on between Barbara and I, it had nothing to do with you, personally. She is my sister. I do share the lose."

Daniel walks haggardly to the door. Not turning around to Helen, he says, "I'll go home and call 911. She is my wife. I belong with Barb."

His words spark a morbid curiosity in Helen. "Is taking his own life hidden in his words." Helen said in A whisper. She lifelessly drops on the sofa.

He closes the door behind himself.

A week later, Barbara, Gravita, and Daniel was buried next to each other. He knew he could not live on without her. After calling 911 he ends his life with his shotgun.

NINE

A year later Helen met Willy Terell Jackson, a new member of Mount Sinai Baptist church. After their formal introduction in the church yard, they agree to meet later at Joe's diner.

Doing their conversation at the diner she learns that he has always prayed for the same things she had prayed for. She wants to tell him not to put too much faith in it, his desires might not be God's WILL. She had, after Barbara and Daniel's death renewed her belief in God. She was shocked to learn that her sister and Daniel had claimed her as their sole beneficiary. Instead, she asks Willy, "How long have you been a Christian?"

"A long time, ever since my late teens, well, outwardly, but inwardly I was missing something important."

"Tell, me. I could be in the same state." She knew something is missing in her life.

"I think I can explain it better if I tell you this."

She leans close--raised eyebrows. "Okay."

He smiles. "One Sunday in church--a different church than I was accustomed to, but the same denomination."

"Baptist?"

"Of course," he replies. "A sermon I had heard many times, but this time, something clicks." He pauses.

Helen was a captor of Willy's countenance and his discovery. "What--?"

"Sorry, I had to be sure I had the right book and everything. The Parable of the Sower: Matthew 13:3-8. I was living on every surface, except the good soil, the seeds fell on, but at different times."

She rests back, remembering the parable, but not its content. It was behind a smoked glass. But still she felt a peace she has not felt in months. -- matter-of-factly, for years. She looks out the large window at her 2006, candy apple red, Mazda Miata and thought of other things she has been blessed with, now this peace. And the preacher's summation: 'God's timetable is different than ours.' She felt the sermon was for her from God. Helen then realizes that God did hear her, and maybe her prayers will be answered, one day. Then another phrase the preacher spoke began to bounce around in her head: 'Where two or more are gather in mine name, there, I am in the mist of them'. Her and John never prayed together. He was a good man but not a Christian. She now realizes how far from perfect their marriage was.

A large smile lit-up her face. I will, forever listen.

"What's funny? I got ketchup or something on my chin?" Willy wipes his chin.

"No." She feels a new life has breathe into her. "I just, feel Good. A strong feeling of Restoration."

TEN

A year and a half later Helen and Willy are married.

A year later Willy and Helen had begun to share their prayer requests. Helen gave birth to a girl, whom she names Gravita Teresa Jackson.

Two years has pass and Helen is yearning for her two boys. Every day she watches Willy express his love to their daughter and less attention to her.

"Am I going to relive that horrible life again. Was naming our daughter Gravita Teresa, an omen?" A siren in the distant. She jumps. She realizes it was Saturday--Willy's home playing with Gravita. For several months now, almost every day when it was time for Willy to come home after work, she'd wait impatiently in the front room, on the sofa, or near the door, praying that he would come home.

May, the next year, she discovers she was pregnant. January, the first, she gave birth to healthy twin boys. They name the first one Willy Terell Jr, and the second, William Terell. At her bedside in the Gaffney Memorial Hospital, Willy holds her hand as he kneels at her bed side. They both thank God for answering their prayers.

Helen's eyes jitter close. Her head drifts to one side and her voice damps to silence as she once again, thanks God for answering all her prayers.

"Thank you, my God, for my *Restoration*." Her hand drops to the side of the bed.

Printed in the United States
by Baker & Taylor Publisher Services